Emmaline

and the

Bunny

Emmaline

and the

Bunny

KATHERINE HANNIGAN

GREENWILLOW BOOKS

An Imprint of HarperCollins*Publishers*

Emmaline and the Bunny
Copyright © 2009 by Katherine Hannigan

All rights reserved. No part of this book may be used or reproduced in any manner whatsoever without written permission except in the case of brief quotations embodied in critical articles and reviews. Printed in the United States of America. For information address HarperCollins Children's Books, a division of HarperCollins Publishers, 1350 Avenue of the Americas, New York, NY 10019.
www.harpercollinschildrens.com

Watercolors were used to prepare the full-color art.
The text type is Bembo.
Book design by Victoria Jamieson

Library of Congress Cataloging-in-Publication Data

Hannigan, Katherine.
Emmaline and the bunny/ by Katherine Hannigan.
p. cm.
"Greenwillow Books."
Summary: Everyone and everything in the town of Neatasapin is tidy, except Emmaline, who likes to dig dirt and jump in puddles, and wants to adopt an untidy bunny.
ISBN 978-0-06-162654-8
[1. Orderliness—Fiction. 2. Cleanliness—Fiction. 3. Individuality—Fiction. 4. Loneliness—Fiction. 5. Rabbits—Fiction.] I. Title.
PZ7.H19816Em 2009   [Fic]—dc22   2008012639

First Edition 10 9 8 7 6 5 4 3 2 1

 Greenwillow Books

For the bunny, unintentionally invited,

who taught me

Emmaline

⋙ and the ⋙

Bunny

⋙❀⋙

Chapter 1

Emmaline wanted a bunny.

She'd seen them on TV and in books.

She liked how they hop, hop, hopped. She liked how they dug holes and scoot-skedaddled under bushes. She liked how they huddled, cuddled, snuggled together.

"What do you want for your birthday?" her mother asked.

"A bunny, please," Emmaline told her.

"Peas or carrots?" her father inquired.

"A bunny, please," she said.

"Five times two equals what?" quizzed her teacher.

"A bunny, please," Emmaline answered.

"One scoop or two?" the ice-cream man wondered.

"A bunny, please," she replied.

Day and night and all year long, Emmaline wanted a bunny most mostly.

All year long and night and day, "Too untidy," she was told.

Welcome to

NEATASAPIN

a very tidy town

*for the stainless, spotless *and squeaky clean*
**wild creatures unwelcome

Chapter 2

Emmaline lived on Shipshape Street in a town named Neatasapin. It was a very tidy place.

Very tidy people lived in
very tidy houses with
very tidy yards.
Even the babies were tidy, mostly.

Orson Oliphant was Mayor of Neatasapin. He was bulky and bad-tempered.

He made proclamations and declarations, mostly.

"I, Orson Oliphant, declare . . . ," he'd begin, big voice booming.

"Tidy homes are spick-and-span sparkling!" he'd holler, feet stamp-stomping.

"Tidy children are still, silent, and spotless!" he'd shout, fists whap-whomping.

"Tidy animals are caged up, leashed up, or locked up!" he'd yell, belly bobbalobbing.

"And the only good weed is a dead one," he'd finish, sneering snidely.

Everyone was afraid of Orson Oliphant, mostly.

Orson Oliphant took a tour of the town. "Not neat enough," he declared. So he put together a plan to make it perfect. "Anything that makes a mess

is banished from Neatasapin!" he proclaimed.

Grape juice and jelly doughnuts had to go. So did spaghetti. Mud pies were forbidden. (Babies could stay, but he made them wear alarms that *beep, beep, beep*ed when their diapers were dirty.)

"No puddle jumping, no skateboard bumping. No snowball whumping or bubble gum chumping!" Orson Oliphant ordered. "And no paints or pudding for small children, either," he said, scowling.

beep beep beep

Orson Oliphant cut down trees. "Leaf litterers," he called them. He had every weed whacked. He covered what he could with concrete. "Much tidier," he decreed.

Then Orson Oliphant rounded up all the wild creatures and sent them away. "They dig where

they shouldn't, they squeak and squawk when they oughtn't, and they scoot–skedaddle where they don't belong," he bellowed.

Even the songbirds were sent packing, because they dropped doodle on cars and other things.

It was a bad time to be untidy in Neatasapin.

Chapter 3

Emmaline was not tidy.

Dirt she dug.

Shrubs she scoot-skedaddled under.

Puddles she hop, hop, *splash*, *splash*, hopped through.

Emmaline yelled, "Hoopalala!" and "Dinglederrydee!" when she was happy.

She huddled, cuddled, snuggled people wrinkly.

Hoopalala!

"Emmaline," her parents would say, "wild creatures dig and hop and scoot-skedaddle. Humans are tidy. Now be tidy."

"I will try," Emmaline promised.

But the next day, there would be some very digable dirt or a "Hoopalala!" happiness, and Emmaline would be untidy again.

The other children would not play with Emmaline. They were too tidy.

"Want to hop, hop, hop?" she asked them.

They looked at her pants splash-splattered, shook their heads, and said, "Only Emmaline."

"Want to dig?" she suggested.

They stared at her arms mud-mucky, rolled their eyes, and said, "Only Emmaline."

"Want to scoot-skedaddle?" She tried again.

They gawked at her hair twig-tangled, walked away, and said, "Only Emmaline."

Then Emmaline said to nobody, "I am always Only. And I am so, so lonely."

Chapter 4

Orson Oliphant heard about Emmaline. He came to investigate.

He watched her hop, hop, hop. He saw her dig and scoot-skedaddle. He heard her holler, "Hoopalala!" He didn't like it.

Orson Oliphant went to Emmaline's parents. "You have a very untidy child!" he shouted, fists whap-whomping. "FIX HER!"

"We will try," said her mother.

"We'll do our best," said her father. (The baby *beep, beep, beep*ed.)

"But—," said Emmaline.

"NO BUTS!" Orson Oliphant boomed. "OR I'LL SEND YOU AWAY WITH THE OTHER WILD CREATURES!"

Emmaline's mother gasped.

Her father frowned. (The baby bawled.)

Emmaline saw they were scared, so she stayed still and silent, mostly.

But as Orson Oliphant stamp-stomped away, Emmaline thought about his threat. "If I went to Away," she said softly, "would wild bunnies be there?"

16

Chapter 5

Emmaline's parents came up with a plan to save her. "If you can be tidy for one month," they told her, "you may have a bunny."

Emmaline's mouth wanted to holler, "Hoopalala!" Her legs wanted to hop, hop, hop with happiness. Emmaline's heart, however, wanted a bunny most mostly. So she said, quite quietly, "I will do it."

Her parents doubted that, but it was worth a try.

Emmaline was determined.

When she saw a puddle, instead of splashing till she was sopped, she stepped around it. She did not slurp-and-burp her soda; she sipped slowly. And when her mouth wanted to whoop, "Whoowhee!" she reminded it, "Bunny," and it behaved.

"Whackadoodlewhipperpoo," she sighed, "this is very hard to do."

It was a mostly terrible month of stillness, and silence, and spotlessness. But somehow she did it. Emmaline was tidy.

Chapter 6

Emmaline's parents took her to the pet shop, where all the animals were caged up, leashed up, or locked up. She hopped once as they walked in the door, because the happiness would not be still.

There were four bunnies in a cage. They were cuddling, head-to-toe and back-to-belly. "Dinglederrydee," Emmaline whispered, because the happiness would not be silent.

The bunnies sat and slept.

Emmaline put her head next to the cage. "We will dig together, we will scoot-skedaddle side by side, we will hop till we fall over," she told them.

The bunnies slept and sat.

Emmaline put her finger in the cage and touched the closest bunny. It was soft like tickles and bedtime hugs. "Oh," said Emmaline.

The bunny opened its eyes. It hopped twice, away from Emmaline. It wriggled back with the other bunnies. It sat and slept again.

"These are very tidy bunnies," the shopkeeper explained. "They sleep and sit, and sit and sleep. They hardly hop, they daren't dig, and they never scoot-skedaddle," he boasted.

Her parents were pleased. "Well, Emmaline, which one will it be?"

"I want a bunny that hop, hop, hops with me," she told them. "I want a bunny that digs and scoot-skedaddles by my side."

"That would be a wild bunny," said her mother.

"That would not be allowed," said her father.

"That would be very untidy," the shopkeeper declared.

Emmaline looked at the bunnies as they sat and slept and slept and sat. A bunny in a cage would be more lonely than Only, she thought.

Back home, Emmaline sat alone. "I am still Only," she said to nobody, "but now I'm *tidy* and lonely."

Chapter 7

Under the big table with the cloth all around, Emmaline made a burrow. In the burrow, Emmaline drew bunnies.

She drew white bunnies, gray bunnies, purple-with-pink-spots bunnies. She named them Bigears, Harry, Petunia, and George.

In her drawings, she hop, hop, hopped with Harry. In her drawings, Emmaline and Petunia scoot-skedaddled side by side. In her drawings, Emmaline and the bunnies huddled, cuddled, snuggled together.

In her burrow, Emmaline was almost not lonely.

One night, the grown-ups sat around the table, and talked over it. Emmaline underneath drew bunnies, mostly.

"I heard," said one grown-up, "of a place that is very untidy."

"I heard," said another, "it has trees here and there, and shrubs there and here."

"I heard," shared a third, "there are weeds everywhere."

All the grown-ups gasped.

Emmaline stopped drawing and listened, mostly.

"I heard," said the third, "wild creatures live there."

Everyone above the table cried out, "Oh," and "No."

"Ah," whispered Emmaline. Then, with a voice

deep and low like theirs, she asked, "Where is this most untidy place?"

"Right around the corner," said one.

"Just over there," said another.

"Past that place but before the other," explained the third.

Emmaline nodded. "Wild bunnies," she said softly.

She gathered the paper bunnies around her. "Dinglederrydee," she told them, over and over.

Chapter 8

$\mathcal{S}$leep Emmaline couldn't. So in the still-dark, she packed a small bag and took a little trip.

At the end of the drive, she turned right around the corner. She went straight to just over there. She passed that place and stopped before the other.

It was just light when she got to Untidy.

It was not a yard. There were trees behind trees, with shrubs in between, and vines tying them tight together. It was a fortress of green.

Emmaline tried to peek in. She poked it. She could not find a way to inside.

"Dungliederrydoo," she sighed. "Now what will I do?"

There was the tiniest *twitch, twitch, twitch*ing by a bush. Emmaline turned to see the twitcher.

It was small and brown, mostly. Its right ear was missing a notch. Its nose was twitching.

It was a bunny. A wild one.

"Ah," said Emmaline, and the notched ear tilted toward her.

The bunny looked at Emmaline.

Emmaline looked at the bunny.

The bunny turned away, and hopped once. It glanced back, white tail wiggling.

Emmaline stepped once toward the bunny. "Bunny," she began.

The bunny hopped two times, and turned to see. Emmaline stepped twice. "Want to," she went on.

The bunny bolted. It hopped so fast its body was blurry. It dove into a hedge, and disappeared.

Emmaline sprinted. Her legs spun so fast they whirred. As she ran she shouted, "Come live with me?"

When she got to the hedge, she plunged into the green. Then Emmaline disappeared, too.

Chapter 9

Under the hedge was dark and scratchy. Emmaline scrunched and squirmed through.

At the other edge of the hedge, there was sunshine. There was more green, mostly. There was the bunny.

"Hello, Bunny." Emmaline smiled.

The bunny turned its ears toward her. It waggled its whiskers, "About time."

Emmaline stood up to see. There were trees here and there, and bushes there and here. There was dirt

to dig, and room to hop and scoot-skedaddle.

"Oh," said Emmaline.

But the trees towered over her. Hoots, huffs, and strange sounds surrounded her. There were weeds.

"This is not like Neatasapin," she told the bunny.

Emmaline huddled near the hedge. "B-b-bunny," Emmaline asked, eyes wide and worried, "w-w-want to l-lead?"

The bunny turned and wiggled its white tail, "Come along." It hopped, slowly, into the green. It stayed close to cover.

Emmaline hopped behind. She stayed close to the bunny.

They hopped in short grass and tall. They hopped around trees and along hedges.

Emmaline watched the white tail go up and down, up and down in front of her. "Bunny," she told it, "I am behind your behind."

When the bunny's ears went out, then in, Emmaline stayed still. "I am listening, too," she whispered.

When there were strange sounds, they scoot-skedaddled side by side. Beneath bushes, they

crouched close together. "Bunny, I am not scared, mostly," Emmaline said.

Under a hedge, there was a hole. The bunny hopped down it.

Emmaline tried to follow. "Bunny," she called.

The bunny hopped out. It waggled its whiskers, "What are you waiting for?" and went back in.

"Bunny," Emmaline called again.

The bunny came out, curious.

"I'm too big for your burrow," Emmaline explained. She sat and considered.

The bunny waited, mostly.

"I know," said Emmaline. "I'll dig a hole next to yours."

Emmaline dug in the dirt. The bunny dug alongside

her. Soon, Emmaline had a hole to sit in. The bunny sat in its hole, on its own.

"Bunny," Emmaline asked, patting the spot beside her, "want to sit here?"

The bunny hopped three times and was with her.

It leaned against her leg. It was soft like tickles and bedtime hugs.

"Bunny," said Emmaline, "with you I am not lonely."

The bunny wiggled its white tail, "No More Only."

"Hoopadinglelaladee," Emmaline told it. And all the best words together couldn't hold the happiness.

﹏ Chapter 10 ﹏

*B*eyond the brush was a meadow. It was warm golden.

Emmaline was cold-shivery from sitting in shade. She hopped out of her hole and ran to the golden warm.

"Bunny, I'm here!" Emmaline hollered.

In the meadow, it was toasty. But there were no bushes or bunny holes. So the bunny stayed still.

"Bunny," Emmaline yelled, "want to follow?"

In the meadow, it was roasty. But there was no cover close by. So the bunny still sat.

Emmaline wiggled her behind like the bunny. "Bunny," she called, "come along!"

Slowly, the bunny followed. Hop, stop, hop, stop, it made its way across the meadow. Far away from cover it went, to be with Emmaline.

Emmaline sat in the warm. She picked dandelions and gave them to the bunny. "Bunny," she asked, "want a bite?"

But the bunny did not nibble.

"Bunny," Emmaline suggested, "let's lie down."

But the bunny sat still.

Then Emmaline rested in the golden.

But the bunny stayed sitting, eyes watching, ears listening, nose sniffing for something unsafe.

Chapter 11

A shadow drew a circle around Emmaline and the bunny.

The bunny's ears went up and out. It sat on its haunches.

The shadow circled again.

The bunny's eyes looked at the sky. Its back leg *thump, thump, thump*ed the ground, "T-t-t-trouble."

Emmaline looked to the sky. A big bird made a circle in the blue.

Emmaline knew about hawks. She'd seen them on TV and in books. They are very fast, she remembered first. They are very strong, she remembered next. They are bad for bunnies, she remembered last.

"Bunny," Emmaline's scared voice squeaked, "run."

The bunny bolted. It headed for cover, far away. The hawk dove. It flew straight for the bunny.

Emmaline, too slow, trailed behind. "Bunny, go! Bird, no!" she shouted.

At first, the bunny was far from the bushes, and the bird was far from the bunny.

It was

bird · · · · · · · · · · · · · · · · · bunny · · · · · · · · · · · · · · · · ·bushes.

But the bunny was fast. So was
the bird. Soon it was

bird ·············· bunny ·············· bushes

bird······bunny······bushes

birdbunnybushes

The bird was at the bunny was at the bushes.

The bunny screamed.

The hawk screeched. It soared up, up, and disappeared.

Emmaline shouted, "Ooooooooooohhh!" The howl of a heart torn terrible.

Then all the creatures were quiet. Even the hoots, huffs, and strange sounds stopped for the heart tender torn.

Chapter 12

Emmaline went to the bushes. She crawled under. She curled up and closed her eyes. "No Bunny no Bunny no Bunny," she moaned over and over.

There was a *sniff, sniff, sniff*ing nearby. Emmaline, startled, opened her eyes to see the sniffer.

It was hiding between branches. Its right ear was missing a notch. Its nose was sniffing.

"Oh . . . Bunny," she whispered.

Emmaline looked long at the bunny. Its eyes were

big and black with fearful fright. Its body shook with heavy heartbeats, *THUNKa THUNKa THUNKa THUNK.*

The bunny did not look at Emmaline.

Emmaline crawled closer. "Bunny, you are very fast," she told it, remembering how the bunny had bolted.

The bunny's big eyes blinked.

"Bunny, you are very smart," she said, remembering how it had not wanted to come to the meadow.

The bunny's body shook.

"Bunny, you are very brave," she told it, remembering how it had come anyway, to be with her.

The bunny's breaths came so quickly.

"Bunny, I am very sorry," she said.

The bunny looked long at Emmaline.

Emmaline opened her bag. She took out two small carrots. She put them in front of the bunny. "Want a bite?"

The bunny's nose sniffed and its whiskers twitched. Its white tail wiggled, "Okay."

Soon, the bunny's eyes were not so big-black. Soon, its heart was not so heavy *THUNK*ing.

The bunny lay on its stomach. It put its ears flat on its head and closed its eyes.

Emmaline lay on her side nearby. She raised her hand. Slowly, she rested it on the bunny, like a blanket.

The bunny's body shivered once, then stilled.

Emmaline felt the bunny's fur. It was soft and warm like summer clouds.

She could feel the bunny's heartbeat in her hand, *thunka thunka thunka.*

The bunny's belly went up and down with every breath.

Emmaline's body shivered once, then stilled.

"Bunny, I would keep you safe forever," she said.

The bunny opened its eyes and looked at Emmaline. It hopped once. Then the bunny lay down next to Emmaline's belly, like they were in a burrow.

While the bunny slept, Emmaline's eyes watched, her ears listened, her nose sniffed the world for something unsafe.

Chapter 13

There was the *swish, swish, swish* of tall grass moving.

There was the *thump, thump, thump* of large feet lumbering.

There were two big boots beyond the bush.

There was a voice. "Come out, child!" it commanded.

Emmaline's eyes were big and black. Her heart shook her with its *THUNKA THUNKing*.

"B-b-bunny, I will k-k-keep you s-s-safe," she scared-stuttered.

The bunny pressed its nose against Emmaline and tickled her. It waggled its whiskers, "It's okay," and hopped into the day.

"Now the human one!" the voice thundered.

Through the brush, the bunny looked at Emmaline. Its eyes were not afraid, mostly.

Slowly, Emmaline followed. Crawl, stop, crawl, stop, she made her way to the bunny. She looked up to see the big-booted one.

She was old and round like the world. She was sun-toasted. She had a long, white braid that crept down her neck, slipped down her side, and stretched out on the ground. The tip curled and flicked, like a tail.

"Why are you here?" the Old One asked. The tail curved a question mark.

"F-f-for the bunny," Emmaline answered.

"How did you get inside?" she wanted to know.

Emmaline glanced at the bunny. The bunny stared at the ground.

The Old One glared at the bunny. "I warned you about humans," she scolded. "They are not to be trusted."

The bunny hung its head.

Then the braid rubbed the bunny's back. "You were almost that bird's breakfast." The Old One sighed softly.

The bunny twitched its whiskers, "I know." It leaned against Emmaline's leg.

"Very well, then!" the Old One bellowed. "Come along!"

She turned and tramped away. The tail trailed behind, watching.

Chapter 14

"Humans," the Old One mumbled, "cutting this, clearing that, concreting everything. They don't care a bunny's hair about anyone else."

Emmaline ran up beside her. "I care," she said.

"You care!" the Old One boomed. "That bunny almost isn't because of you!" The tail shook at her, "For shame."

Emmaline's chin went to her chest. "I didn't . . . I wouldn't . . ."

The tip of the tail touched Emmaline's chest, testing for truth. It sat by the Old One's ear, telling.

"Well," the Old One said, "what's done is done. And the bunny's fine, mostly."

Emmaline started to smile.

"Now you must go!"

Emmaline looked around. They were by the hedge she'd come in under.

"But—," she said.

"No buts!" the Old One commanded. "If you stay, they'll follow. They'll clear this and cut that, looking for you."

Emmaline knew it was true. "Then can the bunny come, too?"

"Child," the Old One sighed. "If the bunny went with you, where would it live?"

Emmaline remembered Neatasapin. Holes would be hated, mostly. "I will make it a home," she said.

"If the bunny went with you, what would it eat?" the Old One wondered.

Emmaline remembered plastic plants and No Weeds Wanted. "I will feed it," she answered.

"If the bunny went with you," the Old One asked, "how would it be safe?"

Emmaline remembered all that concrete, and too little cover. She remembered Orson Oliphant. The bunny could not come.

Emmaline crouched close to the bunny. "I would keep you safe forever," she said.

Then Emmaline cried.

The braid wrapped around Emmaline's shoulders. The tip touched her cheek and took her tears. "Maybe there is something you can do." The Old One soothed her.

Emmaline stopped sobbing.

"You must make an invitation."

"Make a card for the bunny?" Emmaline asked.

"Not a card. A safe place," she told her. "There must be good things for a bunny to eat. There must be dirt to dig, and room to hop and scoot-skedaddle. There must be all kinds of cover."

Emmaline looked at the bunny.

The bunny looked back.

"I will do it," she said.

Emmaline crouched closer. "Bunny," she whispered, "want to watch for my invitation?"

The bunny wiggled its white tail, "I will."

"Now . . . ," ordered the Old One.

"I know," Emmaline answered.

Emmaline took one step to the hedge.

The bunny hopped once behind her and waited.

Emmaline took two steps and turned to see.

The bunny hopped twice toward her.

The Old One picked up the bunny and held it close. The braid waved, "Good-bye."

Emmaline bolted. She dove into the green. Then Emmaline disappeared.

Chapter 15

At the other edge of the hedge, the world was still almost-light. Emmaline did not notice.

When Emmaline got home, it was still still-dark. She didn't stop to see.

She ran to her parents' room. They were still asleep. "We have to—," she hollered.

"Emmaline, it's early," they mumbled.

"We need to—," she tried again.

"Go back to bed," they grumbled.

So she told them, "I went to Untidy. There were weeds and wild animals."

Her parents sat up straight. "What?" they shouted. "When?"

"This morning," Emmaline answered.

"Alone? In the dark?" they yelled.

"It was day. I was with the bunny, mostly," she explained.

Her parents looked through the window at the world. It was only just light. They looked at each other. "Hmm," they murmured.

Emmaline went on. "We hopped together. We scoot-skedaddled side by side. I felt its heart *thunk*ing."

"Really," they replied. "You don't say."

"Now we must invite the bunny!" Emmaline insisted.

"Make a card for a bunny?" they asked.

"Not a card. A safe place," she said. "We need dirt for digging. We need bushes and brush for cover. We need weeds."

"That would be too untidy," said her mother.

"That would not be allowed," said her father.

"I promised," Emmaline pleaded. "The bunny is my No More Only."

"Emmaline," her parents said softly, "the bunny was a dream."

"No!" she shouted.

"Look," they pointed to the window, "it is just now day. So, you see, you were never away."

"But—," said Emmaline.

"No buts," they ordered. "No wild bunny. No invitation. And no weeds."

Chapter 16

Emmaline stayed in her burrow. She did not hop, hop, hop, or dig, or scoot-skedaddle. "It is too lonely without No More Only," she told the paper bunnies. But every day, at dusk and dawn, she sat on the stoop.

One morning, her parents sat beside her.

"You are quite quiet," her mother observed.

"Bunnies are not noisy," Emmaline answered.

"You don't dig yourself dirty," her father noticed.

"Bunnies are very clean," she said.

"You're here every day, early and late."

"Bunnies come out at dawn and dusk," she replied.

"You don't yell 'Dinglederrydee' anymore."

"Bunnies only cry out when they're scared or hurt."

Then Emmaline cried out, "Bunny!"

"Oh, bunny," she cried and sat and sat and cried.

Emmaline's parents were troubled. They sat at the big table, talking.

"Should we . . . ?" they asked.

"Could we . . . ?" they wondered.

"Do we dare?"

They looked out the window at Emmaline, still sitting.

"Yes," they answered, certain.

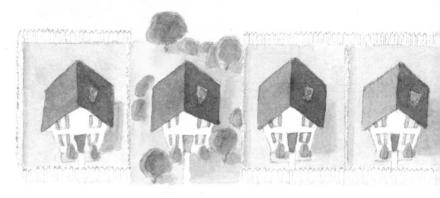

﹏ Chapter 17 ﹏

*H*er parents came up with a plan to help Emmaline. "We want to make an invitation," they told her.

"You want to make a card?" Emmaline asked, barely believing.

"No. A safe place. For your bunny."

"But we will need dirt for digging," Emmaline reminded them.

They nodded.

"We will need shrubs for scoot-skedaddling, and trees and tall grass."

"All right," they agreed.

"We will need weeds."

"We will do it," they promised.

"What about Orson Oliphant?" Emmaline whispered, worried.

"We heard," they said, smiling, "he is hot air, mostly."

Then Emmaline smiled, too.

For the smile, her parents hollered, "Hoopalala!"

Together, they cleared concrete. Side by side, they planted trees here and there and bushes there and here. They watched weeds grow. (The baby made mud pies.)

Emmaline tried it all out.

She dug the dirt. "Very digable," she decided.

She crouched close to cover. "The shrubs are scoot-skedaddly safe."

She hopped around trees and close to hedges. "It is a hop-happy place."

Then she tried the dandelions. "Pa-tooey," she spit a big glob of green.

"What do you think?" her parents asked.

"Perfect," Emmaline proclaimed. (The baby *goo-goo*gled, "I agree.")

Songbirds soaring saw the invitation first. "We accept," they sang. They spread the word.

Squirrels saw it second. "Sure," they said. They set up house.

"I'm glad you're here," Emmaline told them, "but where is Bunny?"

The birds fluffed their feathers, "Sorry."

The squirrels twitched their tails, "We don't know."

So Emmaline waited and watched. At dawn and dusk, she sat on the stoop. Tweets and twitters surrounded her. "I'm not afraid of the strange sounds anymore," she told the world, "but I am still lonely for No More Only."

Chapter 18

Orson Oliphant heard about the yard. He came to investigate.

He watched squirrels scimper-scampering. He heard squeaks and squawks. Leaves littered the lawn, and weeds were everywhere. Then a songbird dropped doodle on his shiny shoe.

Orson Oliphant was furious. "What is this?" he boomed.

"A-a-an invitation," Emmaline stammered.

"A mighty mess, you mean!" he barked.

To her parents he turned. "You have a very untidy yard," he bellowed. "FIX IT!"

Her parents looked at Emmaline. They saw her scared, mostly.

"No," said her mother.

"No," said her father.

("Spthththth," the baby spit.)

Emmaline stayed silent.

Orson Oliphant was not used to hearing, "No."

"There will be declarations!" he hollered, feet stamp-stomping.

"And proclamations!" he yelled, fists whap-whomping.

"I'LL SEND YOU ALL AWAY!" he threatened, sneering snidely.

Then Emmaline's parents made a proclamation. "Orson Oliphant," they ordered, "GO!"

"I'll . . . ," Orson Oliphant sputtered. "You . . . ," he spat. "Ick, ack, oop . . . " Their proclamation had plugged him up.

With nowhere else to go, the meanness blew up inside him. He got bigger and bigger, like a bad-tempered balloon. He turned red, purple, then green with the mean.

"Ah," said Emmaline.

"Ooh," said her parents. (The baby clapped and cooed, "Oh-oh.")

"He is too big!" shouted her mother.

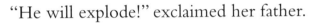

"He will explode!" exclaimed her father.

So Emmaline took a diaper pin. She popped Orson Oliphant, in the patootie.

Shhhhhhhh, the meanness rushed out of the tiny hole. It was fierce and forceful. It sent Orson Oliphant flying.

Whooooosh, he shot like a rocket, high into the sky. Far, far away he went. Then Orson Oliphant disappeared.

"Well . . . ," said her mother.

"What in the world . . . ," said her father.

"Wow," said Emmaline. (The baby *booped*, but didn't *beep, beep, beep*.)

Then they all waved good-bye.

(Orson Oliphant landed in a town full of whap-whompers and stamp-stompers. They whomped and stomped one another every day. It was a hard place to be happy, mostly.)

Chapter 19

*N*ews of Orson Oliphant's flight traveled fast.

"*Yahoo*," the Neatasapinners whispered. They clapped, but quietly and in their closets. They weren't sure Orson Oliphant was gone for good.

By the end of the week, though, Neatasapin was noisy. People hollered, "Hello!" and "How are you?" Children scoot-skedaddled, cheering, "Happyhaladoo!"

They ate spaghetti, with lots of sloppy sauce. Babies

made mud pies for dessert. Small children painted, with pudding.

And on Shipshape Street, songbirds sang a tune. "Tweet, tweeeeeeet, tweet-tweettweettweet" went the song.

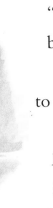

The tweets told the world, "The bag-of-gas bully is bye-bye."

Suddenly, it was a good time to be untidy in Neatasapin.

More wild creatures saw the invitation.

An owl hooted, "Hoo-ray."

Two deer hoofed and huffed, "We'll stay."

A bunch of chipmunks squeaked, "Okay!"

"Welcome," Emmaline told them. Then, "Where is Bunny?"

"No idea," a chipmunk chirruped.

The deer dragged their hooves, "Not a clue."

The owl wondered, "Wh-wh-who?"

"Dunglederrydoo," Emmaline sighed, "now what will I do?"

Still, early and late, she waited and watched.

Chapter 20

One dawn, Emmaline sleep-snoozy sat on the stoop.

There was a *twitch*, *twitch*, *twitch*ing by a bush.

Emmaline turned. She rubbed her eyes, barely believing.

It was bigger and brown, mostly. One ear was missing a notch. Its nose was twitching.

"Bunny?" she whispered.

It tilted its ears toward her. It waggled its whiskers, "Who else?"

Slowly, Emmaline went to it. Softly she said, "What do you think?"

The bunny got up on its hind legs and looked around. There was dirt for digging. There were bushes for scoot-skedaddling. "Nice," it sniffed.

But there were houses and cars *honk-honk*ing. Strange things surrounded it. Eyes wide and worried, it wiggled its white tail, "W-w-want to l-l-lead?"

"Come with me," Emmaline told it.

Side by side, they hopped around trees and along hedges. Together, they scoot-skedaddled under bushes. The bunny dined on dandelions. It twitched its whiskers, "Delicious."

"If you say so," said Emmaline.

The bunny needed a burrow. It started digging.

Emmaline tried to help. Soon she said, "Bunny, I am too big to dig a tiny tunnel." She sat and considered. "I will dig a hole next to yours," she decided.

They dug alongside each other.

When they were finished, the bunny hopped into its hole. Its head peeked out. Emmaline sat in her hole, on her own.

"Bunny," Emmaline began.

The bunny waited.

"You are not a bunny anymore. You are a rabbit."

The bunny waggled its whiskers, "Mostly."

"But bunny," Emmaline went on, worried, "are you still my—?"

The bunny interrupted. It hopped three times and was with her. It leaned against her leg. It wiggled its white tail, "No More Only."

"Mmm," Emmaline hummed, the sound of a heart filled flowing.

Then the chipmunks chittered, the deer hoofed and huffed, and the owl called, "Woo-hoo-hoo," for the heart filled overfull.

Chapter 21

After a while, the bunny's nose nudged Emmaline. "I need a nap." It hopped into its hole.

"Welcome home, Bunny," Emmaline whispered. Then she hop, hop, hopped toward the house.

Emmaline's parents sat on the stoop. She wriggled in between them.

"Is that your bunny?" her mother asked.

Emmaline nodded.

"Does it like the invitation?" her father inquired.

"The bunny likes it most mostly."

"Mmm," her parents hummed. (The baby slept. "Mmm, mmm," it murmured.)

Sitting on the stoop, they huddled, cuddled, snuggled together. They got very wrinkly. They didn't care.

"Hoopadinglelaladee," Emmaline told the world. And all the best words together couldn't hold the happiness.

Acknowledgments

Steve Geck invited me to write a story like the ones I tell. Then he invited me to make the pictures for it. If he hadn't asked I wouldn't have dared it, because it was too dear of a dream.

The cats—Lulu, Winston, and Norbert—introduced me to bunnies. Their introductions were more famished than friendly, but I wouldn't have met the bunnies without the help of these carnivorous captors.

Linda Nebbe, of the Black Hawk Wildlife Rehabilitation Project, told me how to care for cat-kidnapped bunnies.

Professor Lisa Fontaine at Iowa State University first informed me about green printing practices. Justin Tiret at New Leaf Paper, Erin Johnson at Green Press Initiative, and Victoria Mills and the folks at Environmental Defense Fund helped with the tutorial. Ruiko Tokunaga at HarperCollins turned ideal paper possibilities into concrete reality. Steve Geck and everybody at Greenwillow supported using recycled paper from the first. Susan Katz, president of HarperCollins Children's Books, believed printing *Ida B* and *Emmaline and the Bunny* on recycled paper was the right thing to do, and so it happened.

Correcting grammar is no fun, but working with Tim Smith's a pleasure. I hereby dub him "Personal Protector of the Proper Verb of Utterance."

I'm lucky to have the so smart and supportive Debra Orenstein to advise me about all things legal.

For the place I live there is a heart filled overfull, and there are thanks for those who help keep it beautiful.

We care about the health of this planet and all of its inhabitants. So the first edition of this book was printed on 30% postconsumer recycled paper, manufactured by a mill that uses biogas energy.

As a result of these choices, the first-edition printing of this book also saved:

65 trees
24,086 gallons of water
3,088 pounds of solid waste
46 million BTUs of energy (equivalent to half of the electricity used in a year by the average U.S. home)
5,836 pounds of greenhouse gases (equivalent to half of the carbon dioxide produced by the average car in a year)

For more information about recycled paper, visit www.greenpressinitiative.org.

Environmental impact estimates were made using the Environmental Defense Fund Paper Calculator. For more information, visit www.papercalculator.org.